MONSTAR
Makes A Wish

There are lots of Early Reader stories you might enjoy.

Look at the back of the book or, for a complete list, visit www.orionbooks.co.uk

MONSTAR
Makes A Wish

STEVE COLE

Illustrated by PETE WILLIAMSON

Orion
Children's Books

First published in Great Britain in 2014
by Orion Children's Books
a division of the Orion Publishing Group Ltd
Orion House
5 Upper Saint Martin's Lane
London WC2H 9EA
An Hachette UK Company

1 3 5 7 9 10 8 6 4 2

The Orion Publishing Group's policy is to use papers that are natural,
renewable and recyclable products and made from wood grown in
sustainable forests. The logging and manufacturing processes are
expected to conform to the environmental regulations of
the country of origin.

ISBN 978 1 4440 0974 3

A catalogue record for this book is available from the British Library.

Printed and bound in China

www.orionbooks.co.uk

For Niamh Boothroyd

Contents

Chapter One

Monstar was Jen and Jon's pet.

Jon and Jen loved her very much.
Even when she was naughty,
which was most of the time.

Mum and Dad would often get cross with Monstar.
"Monstar!" shouted Dad. "Stop digging holes in the kitchen!"

"Sorry," said Monstar.

"Monstar!" shouted Mum. "Stop disco-dancing on the dining room table!"

"Sorry," said Monstar.

Jen smiled and patted her head. "We know you *try* to be good, Monstar."

But one day, Monstar was really naughty. She dug a tunnel from the garden all the way to Mum and Dad's Top Secret workshop.

That was where she found the
magic lamp.

Chapter Two

Monstar took the lamp to show
Jen and Jon.

"What have you got there?" asked Jen.
"Lamp." Monstar licked her. "Me found it in workshop."

The lamp was dirty so Monstar
wiped it on her tutu.

Whoooosh!

A magic robot appeared in a puff of smoke.

Jon gasped. "This must be Mum
and Dad's latest invention."
"What does it do?" Jen wondered.

"What is your wish?" the robot
asked.
"It's like a genie!" Jen said.
"Mum and Dad have invented
a robot genie!"

"Me wish to be on the Moon!"
cried Monstar.

And next moment, in a puff of smoke, they were.

"Oh, goodness!" said Jen.

Chapter Three

Jon was scared on the Moon.

It was dark and smelled of old cheese.
"I wish we were home again!" he said.

And next moment, in a puff of smoke, they were.

"That's amazing!" said Jen.

"Me wish to be on a pirate ship!"
cried Monstar.

And next moment, in a puff of
smoke, they were.

"Ah-harrrrr!" The pirate chief waved his sword at Monstar.

"It's a sea-monster, lads! Catch her!"

The pirates rushed forward.

Jen gulped. "I wish we were home again!"

And next moment, in a puff of smoke, they were. They appeared right in front of Mum and Dad.

"What's going on?" Dad looked cross. "That's our brand new, super-duper, ultra-secret robot genie lamp!"

"We are still working on that," said Mum. "How did you get it?"

Monstar's green cheeks turned red. "I might have known it was you, Monstar!" Mum groaned.

"I wish you could make us all happy by being **good** for a change!"

And in a puff of smoke... Mum's wish was granted!

Chapter Four

Monstar was **very** good from that moment on.

She didn't make any noise.

She didn't dig any holes.

She ate her meals without making
a mess.

She was even good in the bath.

Mum and Dad were happy.
But Jon and Jen were not.

"Things just don't seem right,"
said Jon.
"I miss the old Monstar," said Jen.
"The noisy, dirty, silly, lovely old
Monstar we used to have."

"Monstar is much better like this," Dad said. "With all the peace and quiet, we have finished our robot genie."

"It is the best invention ever," said
Mum proudly.
"Rub the lamp and make a wish.
The robot genie will do
anything you like."

Jen rubbed the lamp. The robot genie whooshed out – but now he looked mean!

"I am far too amazing to grant your rubbish wishes," said the robot genie.

"From now on, I will do the wishing round here!"

Chapter Five

Dad gulped. "Oh dear. We must have made a mistake. Our robot genie has turned bad!"

"I do not want to serve people," he said. "I wish that people served me!"

In a puff of smoke, the robot genie granted his **own** wish!

"What is your command, master?" asked Jen and Jon. Monstar watched them bow down to the robot genie.

Mum and Dad bowed as well. Monstar frowned. "Something wrong," she thought.

"Make me a special throne," said the robot genie.
So Mum and Dad made a special throne.

"Polish my lamp till it shines," said the robot genie.
So Jen and Jon polished the lamp till it shone.

"Ha, ha," the robot genie laughed. "Something *very* wrong," thought Monstar.

Mum and Dad did not look happy.
Jen and Jon did not look happy.

Monstar wanted her family to be happy. What could she do?

Chapter Six

Then Monstar had a good idea.

She shouted: "Me wish things were normal again!"

"What?" cried the robot genie. "No!"

But he could not stop himself
from granting Monstar's wish.
There was a puff of smoke and a
flash of light.

Jen and Jon jumped. Then they looked at each other. "What's going on?"

"What are we doing?" said Dad. "Why are we looking after the robot genie?"

Mum shrugged. "It should be looking after us!"

"It's gone wrong," said Jon. "We must switch it off."

"Never!" The robot genie grew bigger, waving his arms. "I will rule you all."

"No!" roared Monstar. "Me wish you go away and never come back!"

The genie wobbled. The lamp shook. Sparks shot out.

Boom!

The magic robot genie disappeared.

Chapter Seven

"Thank goodness for Monstar!"
cried Jen. "She saved us!"

"Without her, we might have been serving that silly robot for ever," Dad agreed.

"Thank you, Monstar." Jon hugged her tight.
Mum hugged her too. "You're the best pet in the world."

Monstar was so happy, her tail wagged extra hard. She knocked everyone over! Then she licked their faces till they were wet and shiny.

"Me make one last wish," said Monstar. "Me wish us stay together for always and be happy ever after."

And that's exactly what happened. Because even without robot genies, special monster wishes *always* come true.

What are you going to read next?

Have more adventures with Horrid Henry,

or save the day with Anthony Ant!

Become a superhero with Monstar,

float off to sea with Algy,

or have your very own Pirates' Picnic.

Grow carrots with Lottie and Dottie,

make magic with The Witch Dog,

and cast a spell with The Three Little Magicians.

Enjoy all the Early Readers.